God The Moon
And My Friend Coco

God The Moon
And My Friend Coco

Written by

MARIA PSANIS

Illustrated by

DEMETRA BAKOGIORGAS

authorHOUSE®

AuthorHouse™ LLC
1663 Liberty Drive
Bloomington, IN 47403
www.authorhouse.com
Phone: 1-800-839-8640

Published by AuthorHouse 12/06/2013

ISBN: 978-1-4918-3367-4 (sc)
ISBN: 978-1-4918-3365-0 (e)

Library of Congress Control Number: 2013920394

DEDICATED TO...

God
The Moon
And My Friend Coco

I've been crying all morning and all day.
My sister, Bella, told me to stop crying because
it breaks her heart seeing me like this.
She thinks I'm a mess.
She even asked me if I wanted to go out
and play with her.

Bella never plays ball.
She wouldn't think of getting her dress dirty.
Besides, she never wears jeans.
How is she going to play ball
wearing a dress?

I told her I didn't want to play.
I just wanted to be left alone.
I wish Noah were around but he has
gone fishing with dad.
Noah is my little brother.
He's six years old.

Bella hugged me and told me she loves me
and that she's praying for my friend to get well soon.

I cried more. Bella kissed me on the head
and walked out of the room.
I don't understand why she was being so nice.
Normally she would tell me what to do,
and how to do it.

I walked toward the open window. It was night.
The full moon was looking at me.
I've never seen such a perfect round moon.
It was prettier then my soccer ball.
I stood there mesmerized by its beauty.
Million of stars were covering the sky.
I stared. I was looking to find God.

It makes me wonder . . .
Does God live among the moon
and the stars?
Why can't I see Him?

My mom always tells me
whenever I want to see God
I should look in my heart and there's where
I would find Him.
Does God exist in our hearts?

I have so many questions to ask Him.
Why is my friend Coco in the hospital?
She's only my age.
She's only eight years old.
I was told by my dad
that Coco has cancer and she might die.

Why does God allow for children to die?
Doesn't He know they need
to experience life first before they die?
No one should die young. No one!
Now I'm crying even more.

I jumped out of the window.
The moon jumped with me.
I think the moon is following me.
I reached my arms out to touch it.
The stars seemed as if they were dancing.
The night was dark.

I sat on the grass and I looked up.
Tears rolled down my cheeks.

Why God?
He didn't have the answers.

Next day I asked my mom if I could cut my hair.
She told me that she'd take me to her hairdresser.
She asked me if I would like to visit Coco at the hospital.
I told her yes, after my hair cut.

After my hair cut
I asked my mom if we could stop
so I could buy two matching scarves
for me and my friend Coco.
She said yes.
My mom is the coolest.
She told me that I looked beautiful.

No one ever called me beautiful.

My mom helped me tie the blue scarf with
the pink polka dots around my head.
I looked funny.
"Mom, do I look like a boy?" I asked.
"You're too beautiful to look like a boy," she replied.

I looked in the rear view mirror.
I smiled.

Coco was in the Children's Hospital.
She was on the fourth floor.
Mom was holding my hand as we
walked the long hallway.
There were nurses and doctors everywhere.
I received so many smiles.

One girl came up to me and asked
me if I had cancer, too.
I told her no. I didn't.
She told me I was lucky.
I told her she was beautiful.
She hugged me.

42

She told me her name was Mia.
She had a big scar on the back of her head.
She told me she had a tumor.
I was speechless. I didn't want to cry.
I pulled my scarf off.

I hugged her and told her that
I'll pray for her to get well soon.
She smiled and walked away.
"I like that you don't have hair," she yelled, "You're
awesome! By the way, I don't believe in God," she voiced and
ran down the hallway. "I'm an Atheist!"

I looked at my mom.
I think my mom had tears in her eyes.
"We're looking for room 1113," she told me,
and she held my hand tighter.

"Mom, why do children get sick?" I asked. "Is God the cause of it?"

"No, I don't believe God is the cause of it, Sasha." Mom softly voiced. "God is Love."

"Here is Coco's room, Mom," I interrupted.

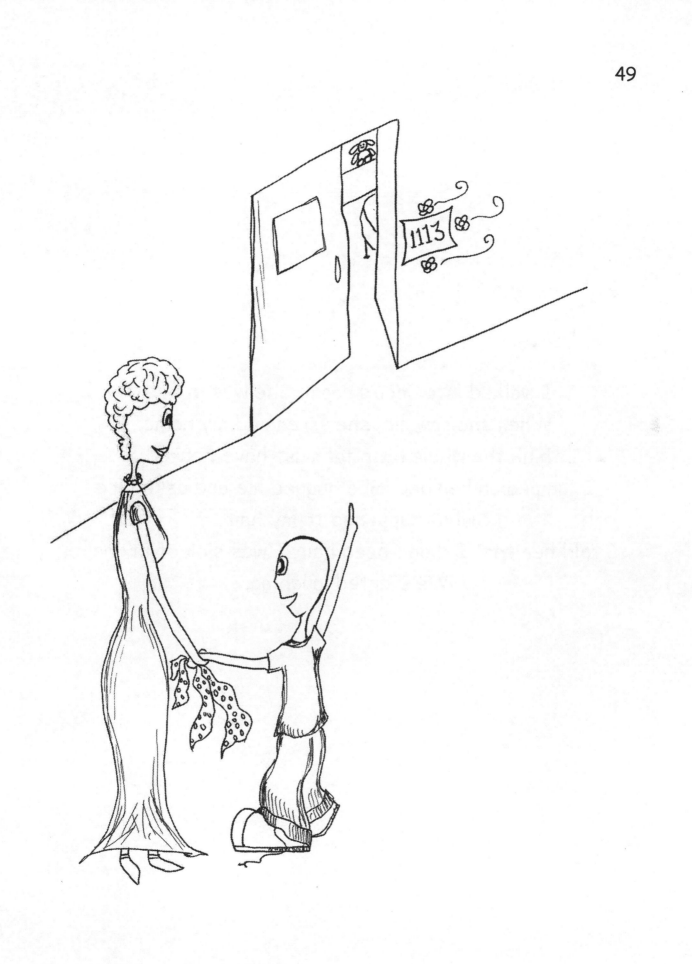

I walked into Coco's room. She was in bed.
When she saw me, she screamed my name.
I think the whole hospital must have heard her.
I jumped on her bed. She hugged me and asked me
what happened to my hair.
I told her that I didn't need hair. I was sick of my hair.
We started laughing.

My mom hugged Coco and asked her
how she was doing.
Coco told her that the best part of being
in the hospital was all the attention she was
getting from the nurses and the doctors,
and she could have all the ice cream she wanted.
Mom excused herself to give us privacy.

Her room was filled with stuffed animals, dolls, and greeting cards. It looked like a toy store.

I reached in my pocket and pulled out the
blue with the pink polka dots scarf.
"I bought this for you," I said, "and I bought
one for me. Look they're the same."

Coco screamed again.
She was so excited and happy.

Coco was bald. She had a big scar on the
back of her head just like Mia.
She had a tumor, but the tumor now is all gone.
She told me she wasn't getting the headaches anymore.

I asked her if she were scared of dying.
She told me she wasn't.
She told me that we don't die.
We just leave our sick bodies and we go
somewhere else, like colorful butterflies.

"How is that possible?" I questioned.
She told me she saw God in her dream.
He told her not to be scared that He'll take
care of her. She no longer was scared.

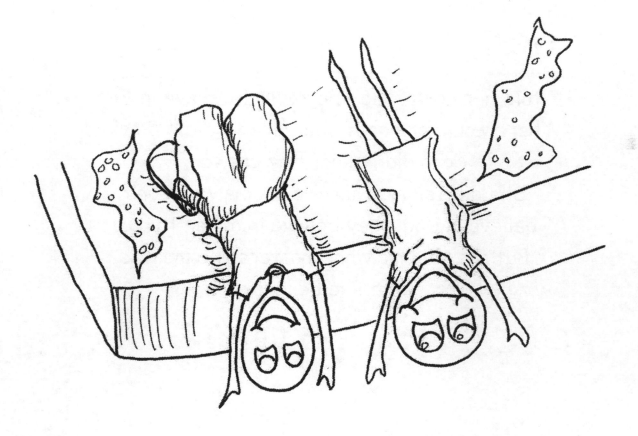

I told her about Mia who doesn't believe in God.
"Where would she go if she were to die?" I asked.
Coco didn't know the answer.
She did tell me there're people who don't
believe in God, they believe in other things.
But she told me what matters the most is
what she believes.

I told her I too believe in God.
I asked her if she wanted to hear
my prayer to God.
She shook her head yes.

I closed my eyes. "Hello God, this is me again, Sasha.
Can you hear me?
If you do, I need to ask you for a favor.
Please, pretty please, don't take my friend Coco,
she's too young to die.
She's my friend and I'll miss her and
I'll cry a lot.
Do you want me to cry?
Just make her well. Use your magic.
Thank you God.
I love you."

"I love your prayer," Coco told me. "Now lets wear our scarves." We jumped from her bed and helped each other. We looked as if we were twins. We looked silly. We made funny faces. We laughed, and laughed.

When mom came back, Coco and I were
laughing and playing with all her stuffed animals.
I was very very sad leaving her.
I told her I'll see her soon.
We hugged and said goodbye.

Back at home that night I jumped out of the open window. I love sitting on the grass and staring at the sky.

A falling star caught my attention.
I've never seen a star falling before.
My mouth dropped open.
Was God trying to tell me something?
I stood up.

I kept looking at the bright moon.
I think they're people living in it.
I moved and the moon moved with me.
Was the moon trying to dance with me?
The stars winked at me and I felt
a soft breeze kissing my face.

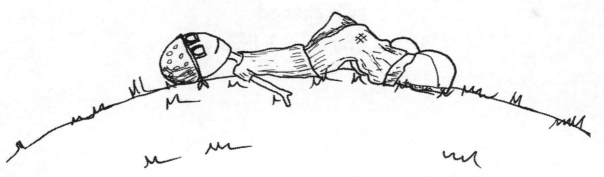

I took a deep breath.

Is God watching over my friend, Coco? I wondered.

"And please God don't forget Mia

even though she's an Atheist.

"I know we're all your children and you love us," I whispered.

"Thank you God! I love you!"